HANSON

CATHERINE MURPHY

ARIEL BOOKS

**Andrews McMeel
Publishing**

Kansas City

www.andrewsmcmeel.com

ISBN: 0-8362-5536-4
Library of Congress Catalog
Card Number: 97-80506

CONTENTS

INTRODUCTION

Zac: Naturally, people are going to think . . . kid group . . . that we don't play, and we don't write and we don't sing, and it's all fake. But it's not.

Taylor: I mean, just listen to the music.

Zac and Ike, laughing: Judge us by our age, not our music. NOT!

In "MMMBop," their first hit single, Isaac, Taylor, and Zachary Hanson sing about friendship. Sow seeds of love and you'll grow friends, the lyrics urge. Some of your seeds will be gone in an "MMMBop" (a word the brothers made up, meaning an instant). But some will grow into roses and be-come the best friends you'll ever have. Which seeds? That's the secret, the part that nobody knows.

What Ike, Tay, and Zac didn't know when they started performing back home in Tulsa, Oklahoma, was just how many friends their joyous music would find them. Now they've got friends all over the world. From Australia to New York, from France to Japan, millions of adoring fans love only one thing more than Hanson's happy harmonies: the awesome young brothers themselves.

It's no secret. Hanson is hot! Music lovers everywhere have been MMMBopping along to the sweet harmonies, soaring melodies, and irresistible rhythms of *Middle of Nowhere*, Hanson's second album. From the seed they planted with "MMMBop," the brothers' musical career has blossomed into an incredible flower—and Hanson is blossoming right along with it.

And the most amazing part? The Hansons are *kids.* When *Middle of Nowhere* was released in May 1997, Ike was sixteen, Taylor fourteen, and Zac just eleven. So who is Hanson, and how did the band climb from the middle of nowhere to the top of the charts? In an "MMMBop" you'll find out—by reading on.

FAMILY ROOTS

For Hanson, everything starts with family, and the Hanson family's a *big* one. Besides Ike, Tay, and Zac, there are parents Walker and Diana, younger sibs Jessica, Avery, and Mackenzie, and a baby due this year. The Hansons are a warm, close bunch. "They don't criticize each other, they don't fight with each other," says Tamra Davis, who directed Hanson's videos. "They were so loving with each other!"

Like love, music runs in the Hanson family. "It's in the genes, I guess," says Ike. Walker and Diana have been

singing ever since they were high school sweethearts. They taught their kids harmony by singing grace at dinner. "There was always a lot of music in the house," Taylor remembers. "Mom would sing around the

house, and then I started singing, and Zac started singing, and so we became a group. It was a very natural thing because there was always music around."

Soon the boys were writing songs as well. "Our parents used to joke that they'd tell us to do the dishes, and they'd

come back and we'd have written a song," says Taylor. "We didn't even think about it, it just happened."

When Walker's company sent him to Venezuela, Trinidad, and Ecuador, the whole family went along. Being Hansons, they couldn't go without music. The boys took tapes of fifties and sixties rock music by stars like Chuck Berry and the Beach Boys, and they loved every doo-wopping note. "These people are the origins for what all music is today," Ike says. "It's just great music."

Back home in Tulsa, the brothers got their act together, singing their own songs, as well as tunes like "Splish, Splash" and "Rockin' Robin." The next step was clear: It was time for Hanson to perform.

A BUDDING CAREER

We started at a local festival called Mayfest," Ike says. At first, Hanson sang *a cappella*—just voices, no musical instruments. But what voices! Their close harmonies and lively dance steps soon made them favorites around Tulsa. By 1995, they'd recorded their first independent album, *Boomerang.* And they'd made a decision. They wanted to play music for *real.*

To do that, they needed a manager, so they stopped music mogul Christopher Sabec on the street at a music conference in Austin, Texas. "We just went up to him and said, 'Can we sing for you?'" Taylor remembers. Sabec remembers it too. "After they sang, I just said, 'Where are your parents? I need to talk to them fast!'" Sabec took Hanson's tapes to at least twelve record companies—all of which are now kicking themselves because they said no.

But instead of getting discouraged, Hanson found ways to get better. "Playing guitar gives you a whole different inspiration," says Ike, "and we needed that different inspiration." With typical Hanson confidence, they got instruments and played them in concert one

week later. "But that
doesn't mean we were good
when we played live," says
Taylor. "It just means we got
out there and did it."

THE BLOSSOM OPENS

I n 1996 Hanson recorded a second album, *MMMBop.* By this time, they were getting phone calls from fans who shrieked, "We love you!" into the receiver—and a major label was finally interested in the Hanson sound.

Steve Greenberg, the Mercury Records exec who signed Hanson, tells how it happened. "I got this

tape and loved it, but I was con-
vinced it was fake. I was sure
there was some adult pulling the
strings. . . . But then I saw them
at a county fair in Kansas, and
they played and sang just as
well as they did on the record.
There wasn't an adult in sight,
except their dad, who was load-
ing up the equipment, and their
mom, who was selling T-shirts."

After Hanson signed with
Mercury, the family spent five
months in Los Angeles while the

boys recorded *Middle of No where* with producers Steve Lironi and the Dust Brothers. Between dips in the Dust Brothers' pool and raids on

their music collection, Ike, Tay, and Zac wrote or cowrote every song on the album.

In March 1997 "MMMBop" was released as a single and promptly topped the charts. At appearances, the boys were mobbed. By the time *Middle of Nowhere* was released in May, Hanson was already a major hit, and the boys were on their way.

IN FULL BLOOM

At Hanson appearances, there's so much shrieking from what Zac calls "the scream squad" that the boys wear earplugs. "We kind of laugh at it, but it's cool to have people respond to you," says Taylor. "The fans are a lot of fun for us," agrees Taylor. Zac's been known to throw autographed CDs to enthusiastic audiences.

Now the Hanson brothers are appearing all over the world—and spending all their time together. Luckily, they like it that way. "Being in a band together makes it even better, because we know each other so well," says Taylor. Of his big brothers, Zac says, "They're like my best friends, only bester."

As they did at the start, Walker and Diana have kept right on supporting their

talented sons—though Walker says wryly, "I never dreamed it would lead to this." Zac's been known to joke, "Our parents forced us into this. Help us!" But Ike says, more seriously, "Our parents have been really good about just supporting us in general. 'Guys, if you want to stop, we'll stop. If you want to keep going and push harder, we'll push harder.' They've just been there to back us up."

As for dating girls, the boys agree that now is just not the time. "None of us have girl-friends," says Taylor. They all agree that there'll be plenty of opportunity for that in the

months and years ahead. "It would be wrong for me to have a girlfriend," says Ike. "Because I'm, like, gone all the time."

Walker and Diana have always homeschooled their children, and going on tour hasn't changed that. "We take our books with us," says Taylor. "The thing is, getting to travel all around—coming to Paris, going to Germany, going to London—there are so many things to see. That's part of school."

But Tulsa will always be home. "It's always nice to be able to come back somewhere that's home," says Taylor. "Even

though New York and L.A. and all those different places are cool, I think Oklahoma is family."

FOR THE FUTURE

As 1997 wound toward its close, Hanson was appearing in Europe, planning a full U.S. tour, and getting ready to make a movie. The boys were having a ball—but keeping their heads. As Ike points out, "You have to remember that this kind of thing can go away just as fast as it can come."

Would the Hanson brothers' wholesome family life, musical talent, and level heads help

them handle the pressures of success? It's a good bet. After all, these young artists

have a spiritual side; they dedicated *Middle of Nowhere* to "the One who plants and waters and causes all things to grow." As Taylor said, "It's not about the fame of the money or any of that stuff for us."

Zac looks ahead. "I hope we get to stay in the music business, and maybe do some acting or directing films or something like that." And Ike

sums it up. "We love to make
music, we love doing what we're
doing. We love where we are,
and we want to keep doing that
in our lives."

A CLOSER LOOK

ISAAC

"It's all very much a learning experience. With every experience, you try to learn a little bit more about what you're doing, and try to do your job better."

Clarke Isaac Hanson, the band's guitarist, was born in Tulsa on November 17, 1980. Ike says he's both goofy and serious. "Though being a kid is kind of a carefree sort of thing for the most part, I guess there are definitely a lot of things that stick in kids' minds." If he wasn't singing, he says, "I'd probably be doing something creative, something artistic."

Ike wrote his first song in third grade. He still loves all kinds of writing—in fact, he's working on a science fiction novel. But he's got moves on the basketball court too. And he's modest about his rise to fame. "It's not about you," says Ike. "It's more about the position that you're in."

TAYLOR

"I wouldn't be me if we didn't sing,
you know. . . . I wouldn't know who
I'd be if I didn't do music."

'm the quietest one, obviously,"
says Jordan Taylor Hanson, and
his zanier brothers agree that Tay's
usually a bit on the shy side. Born
March 14, 1983, in Tulsa, Taylor is
Hanson's lead singer and key-

boardist. He's a talented por-
trait artist who loves soccer,
pizza, animals, and most of all,
music. "All of our friends would
just die to be able to do what
we're getting to do. A lot of
them have never been to New
York or Europe or even out of
their home state. And we're
getting to—not to mention do
what we love to do, which is
sing."

Tay's motto? "When you
want something, it's not that

easy. You have to know what you want and keep going for it."

ZACHARY

MTV reporter, to Zac:
"You're the ham of the group."
Zac: "No, I'm a chicken!"

Zac's the maniac drummer who shrieks without warning, paints with honey and ketchup, and pulls girls up onto the stage to give them T-shirts. "Zac is definitely very crazy," Ike says. "I'm the weirdo,"

Zachary Walker Hanson agrees. "I'm like Gonzo in *The Muppet Movie.*" But he can be thoughtful too.

"I think I'm probably just so shy that I actually just act wacky to make up." Born in Arlington, Virginia, on October 22, 1985, Zac loves Legos, Laser Tag, and math. He says, "I'd like to be a cartoonist if this doesn't work out." But for now, Zac hollers, "I JUST WANNA BE IN A BAND CALLED HANSON!"

WHAT THEY SAY

Part of what Hanson is, is that there's not just one guy who sings. Having three voices is what makes us Hanson.

—TAYLOR

It starts out with being sane in the first place.

—ZAC

It wasn't quite MMMMMM-Bop, and it wasn't quite MMBop, it was MMMBop. . . . It just looked good, three Ms and a Bop.

—IKE

When we first started out, Zac had some old drums that wouldn't stay still, and they would roll across the stage! That was pretty funny.

—TAYLOR

Some people make fun of Hanson. But you know what? I don't give a rip.

—IKE

If music is what you do,
and you love it, why would
you be sad?

—TAYLOR

ke is a girl charmer. He'll always say nice things to girls. It's just something he does.

—ZAC

It's just so cool that all these people are having fun and dancing or clapping to your music.

—IKE

Zac's the drummer, so he'll go, "I'm the drummer, I'll do whatever I want," so he'll speed us up, slow us down, whatever he wants to do.

—TAYLOR

A lot of our songs are really just created. You know, imagination.

— IKE

'm not that great a drummer, but everybody says I can play, so I'll take their word for it.

—ZAC

We were always doing what we loved to do. We weren't worrying about what other bands were doing. We do what we do. And they do what they do. That's the way of the world.

—IKE